dark love

Five Story Collection

dara girard

contents

also by dara girard

Collections

Domestic Disturbance (written as Dara Benton)

The Lady Next Door and Other Stories

Holiday Hearts

School Days: Five Story Collection

Lost and Found

5 Holiday Tales

10 Holiday Stories

Henson Series

Table for Two

Gaining Interest

Careless Rapture

Dangerous Curves

Familiar Stranger

Clifton Sisters

The Sapphire Pendant

The Amber Stone

The Emerald Ring

Novels

Honest Betrayal

the reason why

the reason why

THE CHILD LOOKED FRIGHTENED. But any child might look frightened on that busy night in a crowded gas station convenience store. Carolyn Thomas imagined the child to be about eleven years of age. She couldn't guess the gender from the unisex jeans, blue jacket (perfect for the light chill of a southern Maryland spring), and black baseball cap the child was wearing. She wouldn't have taken much notice of the child if not for the eyes. Frightened brown eyes that seemed almost hollow against the child's honeyed skin tone. But then the child was among what must have seemed like giants—a large fellow near the sodas who smelled like cigarettes and perfume when Carolyn had passed him, two teenagers in thick heeled boots, one confident, the other not; a man in a grey, ill-fitted suit coming or going to work, impatient. He'd looked at his cell phone twice and softly swore at it. The five people who stood in line waiting to pay who she could only identify by the backs of their heads.

Then there was her. But she didn't think a petite black woman with short twists could be very frightening to anyone. Carolyn hadn't grown much since age twelve —to her horror—and at twenty-nine, still got carded when she went for drinks. It was a compliment at times but didn't help at work where few people took her seriously no matter how she modulated her voice. As an orthodontist, it took referrals to build her business since people, when seeing her, assumed she was a dental assistant or a new graduate. But she managed to put them at ease and her professionalism and skill in her chosen profession finally won her patients over.

It was from patients, both old and new, that she'd learned to sense fear. She'd known it growing up. She'd been a frightened child. Frightened of separation, crying every time she couldn't see one of her parents in view; of thunderstorms, burying under the blankets when the thunder roared; of the Boogeyman under the bed; she had her parents use a flashlight to scare it away before they left the room. So perhaps it was just a nervous child she saw and nothing else.

Carolyn glanced at her date, Malcolm Verland, who stood in front of her in the long line after he'd pumped gas into his freshly vacuumed Lexus. He was another adult she hadn't included. To a child, Malcolm could appear to be a little scary—he was a black man of average height with dark, short cropped black hair. His silver rimmed glasses softened his angular features a little, but not much. He owned a portrait studio and liked to brag that he never forgot a face. He even mentioned that he could remember thirty names from the site for Missing and Exploited Children. She found that a rather grim, disturbing interest.

Carolyn sighed wondering why the line felt as if it were moving at a glacial pace. She wouldn't be waiting here if Malcolm hadn't decided to stop for gas on a busy interstate connector before heading to some new Thai restaurant he'd heard about. Why he'd insisted on stopping she couldn't really understand (if fuel had been so urgent couldn't he have gotten the gas before hand?), but she was sure this would be their final date anyway. She liked him well enough but after six months and several outings together there was no spark.

If he was interested in staying friends she'd consider it, but nothing more. They really had nothing in common. It had been more curiosity on her part. She assumed that was the reason why she kept saying yes to him whenever he asked her out. They worked in the same office complex. His studio was one level above her. He was very low key and laid back, she liked to plow ahead. On their first date they'd gone rock climbing, her suggestion not his, and somehow he'd ended up breaking his ankle.

She didn't think she'd see him socially again, giving him an awkward smile when she saw him riding the elevator using crutches four weeks after the incident. But after a couple of weeks, and out of his cast, he'd called her again to see if he could see her, and she'd agreed, more out of pity this time. She had gotten him injured after all and said the second date would be on her. He didn't argue. They'd gone to her favorite seafood restaurant where he'd ended up with a rash because he was allergic to shellfish. He said he hadn't known, she wasn't sure she believed him.

The third and fourth dates hadn't been a disaster (thankfully) but not thrilling either. She didn't really know why she kept saying yes. The third date had been another pity yes. The fourth, probably boredom. A free meal with a nice guy was better than trying to find something to eat at home. But this would have to be the last. She didn't want to waste his time or hers.

Carolyn glanced at the child again. Something about the child's expression bothered her. It didn't just look frightened, but lost. She made a move to walk over to the child then saw the young man next to the child (an older brother perhaps?) nudge the child forward. He had a scruffy look, but didn't stand out. He wore a similar dark cap, his brown hair reaching his shoulders. So the child wasn't alone. Someone was with it. Carolyn sighed, annoyed with herself. She was imagining the Boogeyman under the bed again. It was none of her business.

"Ma'am?"

Carolyn turned to the sound of the impatient accented voice. The man behind the counter reminded her of her Uncle Tayo with his rotund figure and bushy mustache, except he was two shades lighter and wore a turban. Uncle Tayo was unlike the other adults in her life. He wasn't like the ones who used to tease her for being frightened of so many things or the ones who used to scold her for having what they thought of as a silly feminine weakness. No, Uncle Tayo used to tell her that being frightened was sometimes good. That she should trust it. She never believed him.

She believed him even less now, embarrassed that she'd been so lost in her thoughts that she hadn't noticed the line had reached her. "I'm sorry," Carolyn mumbled then stepped out of line and motioned the woman behind her to go ahead.

Malcolm frowned. "What's wrong?"

She blinked. "Nothing. Why?"

"I thought you wanted to get gum."

Carolyn looked down at the packet in her hand as if it had miraculously appeared there on its own. "I did."

He pulled her over to the side near a display of magazines. His tone sharpened. "What's going on?"

She stared up at him, surprised by the seriousness of his voice. She'd never heard that tone before. She bit her lip. *It was nothing.* She didn't want to make a fool of herself. The child and the man would leave soon. "Nothing. Why do you ask?"

"Because you look upset." He sighed. "I know I should have gotten gas before I picked you up. Is that what this is about?"

Carolyn shook her head, vaguely surprised she wasn't as irritated as she had been earlier. "It's not that...it's just...never mind." She chewed her lip, resisting the urge to look at the child again. "You said you had a reservation, right?"

Malcolm touched her arm, his voice patient. "What is it?"

She'd tell him. No matter how foolish it sounded. He would reassure her that it was nothing. Then they'd leave. They'd enjoy a nice meal then she'd stop seeing him. It was all so simple. "I just saw a child who looked frightened, but it's with its brother, uncle or guardian so I'm sure it's nothing."

"You don't sound convinced."

That was also something about him that she knew didn't bode well for a carefree relationship. He was too serious at times. He tended to probe deeper instead of letting things alone. "It's nothing really. Probably just my imagination."

"Where's the child?"

Carolyn turned, half expecting the child to be gone. It seemed like so much time had gone by, she thought the child would disappear (quietly leave the store unnoticed, as if it had never existed). But no...there it was. Still. The presence of the black cap and brown eyes, forcing Carolyn to face her apprehension.

Malcolm replaced Carolyn's pack of gum on the nearest shelf and grabbed a bag of nuts. His movements appeared casual, but when he spoke it was clear he wasn't. "I see her. You're right, something's off."

She didn't want to hear that. "What do we do?"

He swore.

"What?"

Malcolm looked worried. "If I distract the guy do you think you can convince her to go with you?"

Carolyn swallowed. She sensed his urgency and didn't want to ask questions, although her mind was spinning with a series of them. How do you know it's a "her"? Why did you swear when you saw her? Why are you so certain she's in trouble? She wanted to say, "I don't know if I can take her," but somehow ended up nodding her head and saying, "Yes."

It was a bold move. What if they were wrong? What if...?

Malcolm handed her his car keys. "If I'm not out in two minutes, you leave without me and take her to the nearest police station." His eyes held hers. "Promise."

Again she nodded. Too scared to speak.

He began to turn. "Good."

She reached for him, but stopped short of touching the back of his jacket. "Be careful."

He met her gaze and slightly shook his head as if to say, Don't worry about me. Worry about the child.

Carolyn swallowed and lifted her chin ready to do what was necessary.

She watched him bump into the young man then pick up two ten dollars bills off the ground. "Sorry, man. Did you drop this?"

"Uh...yeah..." the young man said. "I think so."

Carolyn felt a little relieved at the young man's greed, it would make things easier. She waited for Malcolm to block the man's view of the child. Carolyn pretended to look at a row of beef jerky as she reached for the girl's hand. What if she screamed? What if she resisted? But soon she felt the child's cold fingers wrap around hers and knew the next step was to escape.

SHE HURRIED to the car under a darkening sky, her nostrils assaulted by the scent of diesel fuel from a passing truck, and put the child in the backseat before she sat in the passenger seat. The girl was trembling and still looked frightened. Carolyn took off her light wrap and put it around the girl's small shoulders. "It's going to be okay. We'll get you to your parents."

The girl gripped the wrapper but didn't respond.

Carolyn looked towards the convenience store and saw Malcolm in the large window still talking. What was he doing? What was taking him so long? Was she really going to have to leave without him? She glanced at her watch. He had thirty seconds left. She looked at the driver's seat. He was taller than she was; it would take another few seconds to adjust the seat to fit her. But she'd drive standing up if she had to. She had to keep the child safe.

Carolyn started to slide into the driver's seat when the driver's side door abruptly opened. She let out a scream of alarm.

"It's just me," Malcolm said, settling into the seat. His tone was grim. "I don't think I fooled him enough."

Carolyn glanced in the rearview mirror where she saw the young man racing out of the store with another customer pointing at their car.

"He knows."

"That's okay." A ruthless grin touched his mouth that gave Carolyn a slight shiver of excitement and unease.

"Let him try to catch me." Malcolm put his foot on the gas and sped out of the station, slipping into the rushing traffic with an ease that surprised her.

They didn't get caught and it took a few miles to realize they weren't being followed. Carolyn felt her pulse return to normal and started to breath normally again. She turned to the backseat. The child's eyes were still wide. She wasn't sure what emotion shone there— fear? hope?

She softened her tone. "What's your name, honey?"

"She doesn't speak," Malcolm said.

Carolyn looked at him. "How do you know that?"

"That's what the alert said. She's been missing for a week. I saw her face in a story I read online."

His grim hobby had a purpose. *I never forget a face.* Yes, he'd told her that and it had appeared to be true. The pieces came together: Why he'd sworn when he saw the child; why he'd known what gender she was and that she was in trouble.

It was nearly a week later that they learned how much trouble Lauren Hollis had been in. They'd spotted her in the busy convenience store just in time. The security cameras outside the store got the perpetrator's license plate and the police were able to track him down eventually.

He was a young man named Greg Jeffers who was on his way to drop the twelve year old girl off in a series of hotels on his way to meet with another man in Arlington, Virginia. He'd come from Delaware to Maryland and had passed, with Laruen in the passenger seat, through two police encounters—both for seemingly harmless traffic violations—but was let go when the well-meaning officers didn't notice the $5,000 in cash, stack of prepaid phone cards and large boxes of condoms as a possible sign of sex trafficking.

Carolyn and Malcolm tried, unsuccessfully, to stay out of the press. But the story of their rescue hit the news —the media amazed by what Carolyn and Malcolm had managed to do, making the incident sound more daring and heroic than it actually was. Carolyn understood the media's interest. It was rare to get a missing kid story to end well, although she knew there would be a lot of healing for Lauren Hollis and for her family.

———

THEY DIDN'T MAKE it to dinner at that new Thai restaurant that night. Instead they stopped by a late night diner and shared a large double fudge brownie with lots of whipped cream. They didn't say much but not much needed to be said. Carolyn inhaled the sweet scent of chocolate and watched Malcolm as he glanced out at the few cars sitting in the brightly lit parking lot and realized she wasn't with him because she was lonely or bored or hungry.

"You're amazing," she said.

Malcolm turned to her startled.

"What you did was amazing," she clarified.

He shook his head looking a little embarrassed. "No, this is all thanks to you. I wouldn't have noticed if you hadn't pointed her out to me." He fell silent a moment, then said, "That's why I like you. You push me to try things."

She smiled. She'd never thought of herself that way. But with him she had tried things she wouldn't have with others. Because with him she didn't feel afraid.

She liked him too. It was a comfortable, settled feeling without sparks, but she didn't need that. Not anymore at least. In a world that could be frightening, she found that something steady, warm and familiar could be wonderful. Malcolm was more than a nice guy who took pictures of families (his specialty being children)—he was kind, compassionate, a thinker, a doer. He'd taken the broken ankle and skin rash better than most. For too long she'd focused on all that he wasn't instead of what he was.

Her fear had made him come into focus.

Fear.

The one thing her uncle had taught her could be good sometimes. Now she believed him. Fear had helped her see the child, helped Malcolm to know something was wrong, and helped her to see him completely.

So when Malcolm asked her if she wanted to go out again, Carolyn didn't hesitate. She said yes and this time she knew the reason why.

the neighbor

the neighbor

HE WAS THERE AGAIN.

Large, intimidatingly male, forceful, unforgettable and annoying. Every time she saw him something bad happened. She was beginning to hate the sight of him.

Anita Cross took a sip of her hot, hazelnut latte, trying to pretend she wasn't tense as she sat among the hiss of the espresso machine, the gentle murmur of voices and the warm scent of coffee beans and blueberry scones. She'd pretend he wasn't there. She'd come here to relax on this late summer day and she would.

She couldn't blame him for showing up everywhere she was. They lived in the same building—on the same floor, he was only two doors away—frequented the same grocery store within walking distance of their downtown apartment in a newly developed area of Stanton Cove, Maryland. They liked the same coffee shop—what's not to like? It was also within walking distance with an excellent selection—even the outdoor courtyard where she liked to sit when the weather was agreeable (on a cool spring afternoon or warm autumn evening)—wasn't out of reach. She couldn't bar him from being in a public place.

But she was starting to wish she could.

Anita took another sip of her latte, casting a glance over at him. Yes, she wished she didn't have to see him. She heartily wished she could prevent him from being anywhere near her because the sight of him meant trouble. Not the metaphorical kind, although he did look like a bad boy with skin the color of black coffee, strong rigid features and a muscular build, but real on-your-guard trouble.

She'd first associated him with trouble when she'd seen his black sedan next to hers at a stop light just before the tire on her car burst, causing her to pull over to the side and call for emergency assistance. She didn't know what she hit, but whatever it was demolished the tire and even damaged the rim. He pulled over too. She told him she was okay, but he didn't leave her until assistance arrived.

The second time she'd nearly gotten run over while walking to the grocery store. She'd seen him coming in the opposite direction carrying a tan colored reusable bag that he swung back and forth, the gesture was more measured than carefree. She'd offered him a brief smile of acknowledgement as she passed him. Moments later, some lunatic who clearly hadn't been paying attention, had driven up on the pavement. He'd gotten her out of the way, she couldn't remember how he'd been able to move so fast, and the car hadn't stopped. It seemed to have accelerated as it left the scene.

She'd ended up with a bruised thigh and scraped arm, but none of that bothered her as she sat on the sidewalk, trying to process what had just happened. She felt hot and cold at the same time, remembering the strength of his grip, the power of his protection as they both toppled to the ground.

She'd thanked him, more angry than scared. He seemed angry too. But she wasn't quite sure how to read his expression; his dark eyebrows were drawn together in a frown. He didn't speak. Didn't even say "You're welcome" or "Are you okay?" He just looked her over, assessed her with the same distant interest of a digital scanner, then looked around them, his gaze sweeping the ground and then the sky.

"What are you looking for?" she asked him.

He pointed to one of the cameras at the intersection a few blocks away. She knew there wouldn't be one on the stretch of pavement where they were. The driver had gotten lucky.

She started to stand then noticed a slow river of purple liquid heading towards her, she quickly saw its source—the bottom of his reusable bag was soaked. She stood and grabbed the bag, angered that her neighbor had also been a victim of the driver's carelessness. "Oh no your groceries are ruined!" She peered inside and saw a shattered glass bottle of grape juice. "We can save the rest of the items," she said, taking out the three frozen dinners. The cardboard exteriors were damp, but she knew the inside would be fine; the cucumber and carrots could be washed and the packet of spearmint gum had been protected by the other items. She transferred his items to the bag she'd planned to use for her groceries. "Here," she said, holding the bag out to him. "Don't say 'no.' I owe you one."

For a moment he stared at her as if he was going to say something, but then nodded, took the bag and walked away.

When he saw her the following day in the elevator, he didn't ask her any questions. Others would likely have asked "Are you alright?" "Wasn't that crazy?" "Can you believe some people?" But he didn't, he just nodded when he saw her, rubbed the back of his neck, cleared his throat, then said, "Umm...your bag—"

"It's yours now. No need to think of returning it, I have plenty of others." She smiled.

He didn't. He just nodded before he shifted his gaze to the elevator doors. She sensed he didn't like her, but couldn't imagine why. Maybe he thought she was overly friendly or pushy, but she couldn't help herself and didn't feel she needed to defend herself either.

It was the following week that made Anita know he was a bad omen. She'd been in the courtyard and noticed him just as something whizzed past her cheek. She didn't know what it was, but it took down a pigeon. She pictured a careless child with a toy gun.

Her neighbor's intense gaze swept the area as it had after the pavement incident, but she couldn't imagine what he was thinking.

"It's nothing, probably some kid with a toy gun or a slingshot," she said.

He didn't look like he believed her, but he didn't argue.

That had been three days ago. Anita couldn't even remember what his voice sounded like. When he spoke, his sentences were always brief and crisp, not enough to make an impression. They had exchanged a few pleasantries, but nothing remarkable enough to be remembered. Not that it mattered.

All that mattered was that the sight of him meant trouble and she wasn't in the mood for it today.

This Friday afternoon, she'd shuffled through her mail, while standing at a dining table she needed to replace, absently wondering if she had anything she could reheat because she wasn't in the mood to cook. She'd ignored a message from her half-sister inviting her over for dinner, something she'd never done before, but Anita hadn't inherited their mother's estate before so Anita surmised that may have influenced her sister's new behavior.

Anita paused when she spotted a letter from her dad. He had annoyingly beautiful handwriting, which just seemed strange nowadays. Who took such care anymore? But he did, making sure his writing was not only legible but also clear and straight as if he'd used a ruler.

His handwriting suited him perfectly—a man with a slender build, alert features and melancholy eyes. "That was my downfall," her mother used to say with a bitterness that never left her. "You have those same eyes.

Sometimes it hurts me to look at you," which may have explained why her mother had started a second family and pretended that Anita didn't exist.

Anita stared at the letter a long moment, then tossed it back down. She'd open and read it later. Her father never said anything interesting. They'd been estranged for years. "Why can't I live you with you?" she'd asked him when she was six, after her half-brother was born. "You're better off with your mother," he'd said and given her no other reason. He'd come in and out of her life like a fog until she'd gotten tired of the uncertainty and the broken promises. During her sophomore year in college, she cut off communication.

Six months ago she'd given him permission to come back into her life, when he'd shown up at her mother's funeral. But instead of phone calls, emails or texts, he'd chosen letters and cards. "Something you can hold on to," he'd told her.

She kept them, but didn't know why and had stopped reading them, because she didn't know how to reply. She felt guilty that she still didn't know how to accept him into her life. He bared his soul to her in his letters, talking about his drinking and depression, but she kept her heart guarded. She didn't want to trust that what he was sharing was real. She didn't want to be hurt in case he disappeared again.

Anita absently shuffled through the rest of her mail then decided to go to the coffee shop. She knew it wasn't because she didn't want to cook or that she was really in the mood for a latte. She wanted to escape her father's letter and the words she wasn't ready to read.

The seemingly harmless envelope seemed to whisper to her to open it. To read what was inside. To let it—them—because there were others—become part of her life. But she wasn't ready. Later. She'd get to it—them—later. Right now she needed to be somewhere else.

The coffee shop was supposed to be her refuge.

But he'd shown up.

Or perhaps he'd been there and she hadn't noticed him at first. It was only when she'd taken a seat near a window and looked around that she'd spotted him sitting in a dark corner. The coffee shop was brightly lit, so she wasn't sure how he created the effect, but he seemed to be in shadow. He sat at a round table with a small brown paper cup with a white lid and a pair of keys placed next to it. He always sat alone with his back to the wall. He looked around as if on high alert. Always watching, not on edge, but with a cool, detached observatory air.

Maybe if she ignored him nothing bad would happen. What could happen in a coffee shop?

———

EVERY TIME HE SAW HER, his mouth refused to move. Karim Harlow glanced at his neighbor then looked away feeling as awkward as a kid at a peep show. It wasn't because she was beautiful, she wasn't. But she was striking with her cocoa brown skin, dark twists, which she gathered into a bun at the nape of her neck, full lips and soft cheeks. She was easy on the eyes, but that wasn't what left him tongue-tied. It was just one moment that changed it all for him. She probably didn't even remember the incident, but it was etched in his mind.

It had happened three months ago when he had only been living a week in his new place and had finally cleared enough boxes to invite his sister to visit. He wanted enough space for her wheelchair to move around. He was teasing her about something, he couldn't remember what, but if he'd been paying attention he would have noticed Anita getting into the elevator with them. All he remembered was hearing a surprised gasp and then, "My alma mater? What are you studying?"

He turned and saw Anita pointing to his sister with a vibrant friendliness, he rarely saw. Few people were that kind to her. Although her mind was bright, her body was contorted by cerebral palsy. Most people looked away, but Anita was staring at the UMBC sweatshirt his sister proudly wore and instead of assuming it was just a souvenir thought his sister was a student at the university.

His sister replied, true delight evident in her tone and he learned that Anita was a science tutor and even offered her services. The elevator ride ended too soon and before he knew it she was waving and walking down the hall to her apartment.

For the rest of the visit it was his sister's turn to tease him. "I know you like her," she said while they shared a pizza in his living room. The only place that was suitable for visitors.

"I don't even know her."

"That's what dates are for."

"She's probably seeing someone."

"You won't know if you don't ask."

That was the problem. He couldn't manage to open his mouth to say anything. When he bumped into her at the grocery store he could only manage a grunt; in the courtyard a semi-civil nod. He couldn't understand his fear. The Marines had taught him how to think, act and take charge. He'd faced battle. He now owned a successful security firm. Give him a problem, a mission or a job and he was fine, but without it he was lost. Why was talking to her so difficult?

And then there were the accidents. The near miss made speech even worse. Her car tire didn't look like it had hit something. It looked as if it had exploded, but she'd never mentioned anything, and he was sure she wasn't the type to keep thoughts to herself. If her mechanic had told her something bad, she would have let him know.

He'd expected her to say something about the tire. Instead she'd been her regular cheery self.

Then there was that damn car. He'd been so angry when the tan colored Acura nearly ran her down, words didn't come. He wanted to say more—he wanted to say something, *anything*—but they stayed trapped in his throat. Just as they had in the courtyard. He'd searched for the pigeon that had been hit to see what had struck it, but it had disappeared. It must have only been stunned and flown away or moved, which wasn't good. He couldn't imagine anyone hurting her. He wanted to keep her safe.

That's why he watched her. There was something not right about the three incidents. He'd noticed the license plate of the car—Florida tags, looked like a rental, but he didn't get the full plate number.

He also sensed he wasn't the only one watching Anita. Today, Karim noticed a man—nondescript with a habit of chewing on his bottom lip—in a booth, also watching her. He'd seen him before, passing by the court-yard and in the coffee shop. He usually came with another man equally nondescript, except white. He'd seen them twice before, behaving like business colleagues instead of friends. But this time the man was alone and that bothered him. He didn't know why, but his gut said he had to do something and he always trusted his instincts.

He took one last swig of his now cold coffee. He had to do what at first had seemed impossible. He was going to have to talk to her.

———

ANITA WATCHED him take a drink of his coffee then frown. She didn't know his name—or had forgotten it, which was possible—or even what he did for a living. They'd been neighbors for a couple of months and all she knew was that he had a sister with a great laugh who was studying microbiology. Again, it didn't matter. She didn't need trouble today. She had enough on her mind. She was going to enjoy her drink and forget all about him. She closed her eyes and lifted the warm cup in her hands, bringing it close so she could inhale its aroma.

The sound of a chair scrapping across the ground jolted her out of her peaceful moment. Her eyes flew open. She looked up and saw him. He loomed over her like a dark shadow, although today he wore a light brown jacket and jeans. She stopped with her cup halfway to her lips.

"This is what you're going to do," he said in a low voice. "You're going to put your cup down and follow me outside."

Was he insane?

His tone sounded serious; his look even more so. And his voice. This was the most he'd spoken to her. She almost wished she hadn't heard it. Deep and deadly. She looked down at her cup, she could throw it in his face. It would be hot enough to give her time to run.

"I'm here to help you," he continued. "Now slowly stand and I'll explain. There are plenty of people on the street. You won't be alone with me and it's safer there."

Safer? It didn't seem that anywhere was safe with him. What could be wrong with where she was?

"Anita, please, we don't have time."

How did he know her name? Had she told him? Maybe she'd mentioned it to his sister. He'd remembered it? Why couldn't she remember his?

"Do I have to leave my drink?" she asked. It was an inane question considering the bizarre situation, but she wanted to have a semblance of control and the warm cup gave her courage.

He thought for a moment then said, "No."

He held out his hand.

She took a deep breath. Trouble. She knew it.

———

HIS PACE PICKED up once they were outside.

She heard the shout of a man saying goodbye to a friend dropping him off at the curb, the easy flow of traffic, and her latte felt cool compared to the summer sun.

He headed back to their apartment building.

"Will you tell me what's going on?" she asked him, his pace and her unease making breathing difficult.

"I'm not sure yet."

He walked inside the main entrance. She headed for the elevators. He shook his head. "We're taking the stairs."

Seven floors. She wished she'd left her coffee at the shop. Her neighbor—damn, what was his name?—looked like he ran twenty miles a day and would be up to the task; the extent of her daily exertion was jumping in and out of a shower. Winded, she finally reached her floor. "This is ridiculous," she said her temper peaked. "Is there someone following me?"

"I'm not sure."

"Then why..."

She paused when he put a finger to his lips. He

looked down the dark blue carpeted hallway, then motioned her to stay put. She nodded. He walked towards her apartment door. A few moments later he returned to her, looking grim. "Did you lock your apartment?"

"Of course."

He nodded, his expression becoming even more grim than before. "That's what I thought."

"Why?"

"It's unlocked."

"What!" She headed towards her apartment, but he grabbed her arm, stopping her. His grip didn't hurt, but the gesture surprised her. She turned to him and saw a holster underneath his jacket. He carried a gun. Somehow that didn't surprise her. She raised her eyes to his face and she didn't know what showed on her face, but he quickly let her go.

"No, stay here," he said. "Let me check it first." He handed her his keys. "Go to my place and hide. Do not come out unless you hear the sound of the microwave."

"But—"

"Anita."

He said her name, but the meaning was "Just do it and don't ask questions I can't answer yet."

She sighed. "Should I leave the door unlocked?"

"No. Now go."

He must have an extra key. Should she believe him? Trust him? What if it was all a lie? Why would he lie? What if there were just burglars? But the tone said much more.

"Was the door damaged?" she asked, using the same hushed tone he did.

"No."

"Can I see?"

"From a distance."

She inched forward and saw the door ajar—strange that they'd pick the lock to her place.

"You've seen. Now go."

She turned and hurried to his apartment. She didn't give herself much time to look around, although from her brief assessment it suited the man. Neat, orderly without much color. She thought of dumping her drink down the sink, but didn't think she had the time and didn't want to leave it out in the open, so she quickly shoved it into his fridge. When she closed the fridge door, she saw a business card with the words *Harlow Security* on it and a quickly scrawled note that said "For Karim," ah yes, that was his name, she thought with satisfaction before she hid in the back of his bedroom closet.

Hours seemed to pass and there was no sound of a key in the lock, no footsteps, no sound of a microwave. What was going on?

She thought of emerging from her hiding place and confronting him.

Then she heard footsteps, they paused, retreated then headed forward again. Seconds later she heard a grunt then a thud.

A few more seconds passed before she heard the 'ding' of a microwave.

Anita cautiously made her way out of the closet, then

his bedroom. She stopped when she entered the hallway and saw an unconscious man on the ground. Karim secured his hands. He glanced at her over his shoulder then said, "Do you know him?" He lifted the man up by the hair.

Anita looked at the bruised face and shook her head.

Karim took out his cell phone and held the screen out to her. "How about him?"

She stared at the image of another bruised face and again shook her head. "But—"

He hefted the man over his shoulder. "Give me a minute while I take the trash out," he said then casually left as if he were doing just that.

———

"Do you have any enemies?" Karim asked as they sat facing each other in his living room.

"Not that I know of."

"Someone doesn't like you. I saw it first when someone tried to take out your tires."

"My tires?"

He nodded.

"And that car that nearly ran me down wasn't an accident?"

He shook his head.

She blinked. "But that doesn't make sense. I'm a science tutor for crying out loud."

"Perhaps an angry parent? A child who failed?"

"All my clients succeed," she said trying not to sound

affronted. "None of them would want to hurt me and I get most of my business through referrals."

He sighed. "Well, someone doesn't like you."

"What were they looking for?"

He rubbed his chin. "That's what I can't figure out. Your place wasn't trashed. They were waiting for you. At least one was. That's what made me suspicious. The two were usually together, but at the coffee shop I only saw one. That's when I thought one may be at your place. It's likely the first one saw us leave together and followed us. I caught him by surprise before I faced the second man."

"That makes sense."

He shook his head in disagreement. "But there are still too many questions. It may take more time for me to get information out of them."

"You mean you didn't call the police?"

"I will once I get what I need," he said in an even tone.

"Where did you put them?"

"They won't hurt you."

That wasn't what she'd asked, but his tone made it clear he didn't plan to give her a straight answer. "Can I go back to my place?"

He stared at her for a long moment, the same assessing look that made her feel tense, then nodded. "I'm coming with you."

———

HER APARTMENT DIDN'T LOOK like it had been robbed; it looked like it had been destroyed. Anita saw her dining room table lying on its side with a leg missing, her mail scattered on the ground. A dented lampshade sat on the couch, missing the body of the lamp, her couch seemed to have been shoved several feet from its original position.

Anita shook her head confused. "I thought you said my place wasn't trashed."

Karim cleared his throat. "I caught him by surprise and he wasn't willing to leave so I had to persuade him. Sorry, about the mess."

It was an odd thing to say considering he'd saved her life, but she didn't make fun of him. She just shrugged. "It's okay, I needed to redecorate anyway." She gathered up the letters, and saw a drop of blood on her father's envelope. She glanced at a side table and saw an empty space where a purple and blue glass vase use to sit. She saw small shards on the ground. He'd tried to clean up, which explained why the bottom half of the lamp was missing. What a strange man.

He noticed her glance and said, "Just tell me how much it cost and I'll—"

She shook her head. "It's okay, I told you that."

A muffled noise from somewhere down the hall, made him stiffen and go on alert.

Anita tensed.

Karim pulled out his gun. "Go back to my place."

Before she could do anything, a tabby cat let out a loud cry before it dashed across the room.

Karim looked at her. "I didn't know you had a cat."

"I don't," she said and with that she saw Karim's face change as he looked past her. With lightning speed he dived for her as a loud sound pierced through the air. He covered her body with his as he had last time, but this time she felt pain radiate through her body, down her leg as she hit the ground. She craned her neck and saw a man, staring at them with dead, soulless eyes and saw something familiar on his wrist. But only for a split second because Karim took him down with one shot. The man collapsed to the ground, holding his left shoulder and swearing.

Karim walked over to him. "Only your mouth is allowed to move."

The man said something crude and reached for his gun.

Karim pulled the trigger again, hitting the man's arm, shattering his humerus and he went still. "Damn, the cat must have wandered in, I didn't think—" He turned to her then his face paled.

She didn't know why at first until she followed his gaze to her leg. She looked down and saw blood spreading down her thigh. She wasn't afraid, she was glad to know why she hurt so much.

He rushed over to her, fell on his knees and swore. "He got you. I'm sorry." He grabbed a cushion and pressed it against her leg. "Hold this there until I get back." He ran down her hallway and she heard a door open before he came back with towels and tied one around her leg.

"You're going to be all right," he said more as a

command than as assurance. His tone said "You're not allowed to die," and she wanted to listen, but her body felt heavy as if every time her heart beat her breathing slowed. She knew he'd called the ambulance, she'd heard him, but she also knew there wasn't much time.

"The...watch," she said.

"What?"

"The man works...for my...brother. He gives out...watches like that ...to his top employees."

"Okay."

"Tell the police in case..."

"You'll be able to tell them yourself."

Anita felt a little guilty. This was the most she'd ever spoken to him and at such an awful time. She'd been the one with trouble following her, not him. He must have thought she was cursed. Now she was glad he was always there. Each time. Every time. He'd protected her. Now she wanted to know everything about him. Not just that he operated a security firm and liked to jog no matter how cold the weather. She wanted to know whether he liked his eggs scrambled or sunny side up or even if he liked eggs at all. Her heart turned over and a warm glow spread through her as she studied him, wanting to remember every feature of his face, the slope of his nose, the shape of his arms.

"I love you," she said, because she wanted to love someone. She'd kept her heart closed up for so long and she didn't want to miss this chance. To be real for once. If this was her last moment, she didn't want to waste it.

"I love you too," he said softly.

She didn't believe him, but was glad to hear it. Was he saying what a dying woman needed to hear? Did he pity her? Did it matter? A tear escaped and slid down the side of her face.

"Since the first time I saw you," he said his voice barely a whisper. He brushed her tear away, and his hands were rough, but she didn't care. It felt good to love him and to be loved. If she lived, she'd never waste another moment again. She shifted her gaze to her father's blood stained envelope, wishing she'd opened it.

———

KARIM SAT in the hospital cafeteria where Anita had been for the past four days. The bullet had ripped through a major muscle. She'd made it through surgery, but there would be grueling months of physical therapy. He'd visited her only once, with her father, but she'd been groggy and probably didn't remember. He frequently came to the hospital to check on her progress, although he didn't see her. He'd wanted to visit her every day. Every minute of every day, but he stayed away as much as he could. He didn't know what they could call their relationship yet, not even sure they had one. She'd told him she loved him. But what she'd said had come from shock. He knew people would say anything when facing death. He didn't want to press her to feel something she didn't. He remembered seeing her cup in his fridge, he should have thrown it out, but hadn't yet.

He also stayed away because it hurt too much to see

her. There were so many other choices he could have made to keep her safe. He replayed them in his mind.

"This is your chance," his sister had told him through a video chat session. "Tell her how you feel."

"She already knows."

"You're always too hard on yourself."

He knew that. It didn't change anything or make him feel any better.

"The biggest problem with you is that you're only comfortable in battle or when you're on alert. Taking charge, giving orders. You need to know that the quiet moments can be just as powerful."

"I know that."

"Then stop being afraid of saying the wrong thing. It may feel like life or death, but it's not."

She should know. He remembered her speech therapy sessions, the way the kids would make fun of her at school. She still continued to joke and talk no matter the sting. That was bravery, she taught him that every day. He had no excuses.

"What should I talk to her about?" he said.

"Oh...maybe that her brother hired three hit men to kill her so that he could get her inheritance?"

He frowned. "I'm not going to bring that up."

"It made the news. It's a juicy story."

"I'll find something else."

"Good. As long as you do."

———

Anita stared at the cooking demonstration on the TV attached to the corner wall of her hospital room. She still couldn't believe her half-brother had tried to get her killed. She'd guessed when she'd noticed the watch, but it was only when one of the hit men Karim had tied up and stuffed in the utility closet had started talking that all the pieces fell into place. Her brother had given them each a chance, raising the stakes each time they failed so that they'd become more committed to her demise. The first attempt had been a bomb that hadn't detonated properly. They'd bribed the mechanic to lie about the cause of the damaged tire. Karim had disrupted their second and third attempt. That day in the courtyard, if she hadn't turned to look at him, the bullet would have hit her instead of the pigeon.

It was the third hit man, who stayed out of sight giving Karim the impression there were only two of them, who thought to kill Anita in her apartment. They'd hoped to stage it to look like she'd come upon a burglar, but Karim had ruined their plan.

However, the third guy had been determined to use surprise as his strategy. After Karim had encountered the second man in Anita's apartment, he'd remained hidden, ready to shoot Anita when she returned, determined to get the fifty thousand her brother had promised.

It didn't seem like much to take a life, but she didn't know his circumstances nor care.

All she knew was that greed had turned a happily married father of two into a killer. Her half-brother wanted to gain the entire inheritance. He'd gone through the money his father had loaned him to start his club marketing enterprise where he'd over expanded and was bleeding red every week. He hoped his mother's money would save him.

But she hadn't left him anything, except some jewelry and ornaments she'd hoped he would give to his daughters. He'd pawned them instead, angered that their mother had given Anita everything he thought mattered. Anita had never felt easy about her mother's decision, feeling the weight of her mother's guilt instead of her love. Her mother had foolishly written in her final decree that she hoped by giving Anita the money she could have a closer relationship with her half-siblings. She'd been wrong. Her half-sister still called, but their relationship was just as uneasy as before. Perhaps time would change that, she wasn't sure.

Her father came to visit her in the hospital. And he read to her.

Karim visited her too, but only twice. "I don't want you to focus on what happened," he said, never mentioning he told her that he loved her. She remembered the brief touch of his hand. "I want you to focus on getting better. I'll give you space until you're ready."

She didn't tell him she didn't need space. Didn't want space. That he could visit her every day, but she hadn't had the strength to fight his formal, distant words. And part of her wanted him to wait until she was stronger. She didn't want to be a reminder to him of what could have happened. She saw the uncertainty and guilt in his gaze and knew it would take time for it to fade. Yes, he could have kept her at his place; yes, he could have moved faster, but he hadn't and that was okay. She didn't need him to be perfect. She didn't want him to see her as weak. She didn't want this awkward silence between them.

But she did want to see him again.

She went through two months of physical therapy for her leg. She used a cane now, but in a few days she wouldn't need it anymore. She shuffled through her mail then smiled when she saw her father's handwriting on an envelope. She ripped it open and saw a quote: "When the choice is now. Tomorrow is too late." Then in his beautiful lettering he wrote, *Don't be shy to make the first move.*

She'd shared her uncertainty with him, and he'd given his response. It was just the nudge she needed.

Anita put the letter down and went to Karim's apartment. She knocked and waited, but no one came to the door. She glanced at her watch. She knew where he would be.

But he wasn't there.

There was the same hiss of the espresso machine, the gentle murmur of voices, the scent of pumpkin spice muffins, but he wasn't there.

Anita let her eyes sweep around the coffee shop once more, moving aside from the doorway when a couple bundled up as if they were going to the North Pole instead of outside into the crisp winter air, needed to exit. She'd hurried there, hoping to see his shadowy frame in the corner with a cup on the table and his keys. But the table was occupied by three teenagers wearing the same dark rimmed glasses, one had a buzz cut with pink tips.

Anita sighed, walked to the counter and ordered a cinnamon latte and muffin. Too late she realized her mistake. Carrying a tray would be hard with a cane. She managed to balance the muffin on top of her coffee as she slowly walked to a table. She rested it down with satisfaction and waited.

He still didn't show. The one face she was looking for, the one person she wanted to see, wasn't there when she most wanted him to be. She ate slowly giving him plenty of time.

He still didn't show.

After an hour, Anita finished her drink and muffin then left, favoring her right leg, although her left was getting stronger. But she was feeling a little sorry for herself. Maybe it had all been just words. Maybe he regretted what he'd said that day when she'd been shot. It had been dramatic and emotional. Even in the hospital there had been an awkward tension time should have lessened.

But perhaps it hadn't. Nobody needed this much space. She hardly saw him anymore. She didn't bump into him in the grocery store or in the courtyard. In the hallway he was always in a rush, he'd give her a brief cordial wave then take the stairs instead of the elevator.

Maybe just as she'd once hated to see him, he now felt the same.

Anita stopped walking when she heard running footsteps behind her. She spun around too fast, putting pressure on her bad leg. She lost her balance. He caught her before she fell.

"Did you just come from the coffee shop?" he asked, his breath coming out like a mist in the cold air.

She nodded, blinking back tears. She didn't want him always coming to her rescue. She didn't want him to think he needed to.

"Were you waiting for me?"

She nodded again unable to speak, so many thoughts swirling in her mind.

"Things got busy at work. I'd wanted to be here," he said, ducking his head.

And that's when her tears dried up and her worry fell away, her heart renewing with hope. He was shy. She'd never thought of that, never imagined that his silences could be anything but cold detachment. She stared at him with the same eyes of love that she had two months ago. She knew what he needed. If he was shy, she could be bold.

"Sorry to make you wait, I—"

She didn't let him finish, kissing his words away. His lips felt cold and he smelled like spearmint. She didn't need him to apologize. He was there now.

And now was all that mattered.

dorcas

dorcas

Everybody knows that Dorcas Mortag burns everything she touches. If you want your house to still be standing you wouldn't let her set foot in your kitchen. She could burn water if given the chance. But she was never a bright woman—not thick mind you, just not brilliant. I don't say this to be mean. I say it because it's true. I found out how true it was when I made a foolish promise to her over forty years ago.

Secrets are hard to keep. I know. I've never been able to keep one, which is why people don't tell me things and I don't want them too. I have plenty of my own business in which to manage and I don't have time for someone else's mess cluttering up my mind. Promises are also hard to keep, but, unfortunately, easier to make. That's what got me into trouble. I'd made a simple promise a long time ago, never thinking much about it until I was asked to honor it.

It was little comfort that I wasn't the only one who'd

made this promise. We were three girls of twelve when we made our binding vow. I remember it was a rainy day in Port Antonio. My mother had gone to the shop and I was looking after my little sister when Dorcas, Aletta and Terry stopped by.

Dorcas wasn't much to look at, although she was best friends with her opposite, Terry, who had looks that had turned heads since the age of five and she had wealthy parents. Terry was cheery, small and kind. Dorcas was big and sweet. On the other hand, our friend, Aletta, had a face that looked like a truck had backed over it several times. People whispered that she'd come into the world crying and had never found a reason to smile. She was usually irritated or miserable, but she was clever and helped us with our homework, which was the main reason why we kept her in our circle.

They came to my house because I had the most space and adults were not usually around. My mother was always working. I didn't know where my father was--or to be honest *who* he was--and my uncle, who had a room down the hall, was always leaving some woman's bed before her husband showed up. That day, aside from the light patter of rain, I remember the smell of fish fritters and sorrel juice I'd made for my sister. Aletta sat and lit a cigarette.

I snatched it from her and stomped it out. "Yuh mad? You can't smoke here."

"Mi sorry," she said not sounding sorry at all.

I didn't let her attitude bother me as long as she didn't dare try to smoke again. My mother could smell the residue of anything—liquor taken from her cabinet, another woman's perfume on her boyfriend's shirt and *definitely* cigarette smoke in her prized sitting room.

"I want you to do something for me," Dorcas said. She had a sweet voice like pink candyfloss or an ice lolly. She could make you forget that sometimes what she said made no sense. "I want you to promise to lie for me."

"Why?" I asked.

Aletta scrunched up her face. "Lying is a sin."

"Not all lies," Dorcas said.

"Yes, they are." Aletta held her hand out. "Get me a bible and I'll prove it."

"She's right," I said. "Sometimes you have to lie."

"You should never lie."

I folded my arms and glanced at the bag where Aletta hid her cigarettes. "What do you tell your sister when her fags go missing?"

"I don't say anything."

"That's the same as lying."

"Why promise to lie for you?" Terry asked Dorcas before Aletta could challenge me.

Dorcas lowered her voice as if she were sharing a secret. "I want you to promise me, just in case I do something bad."

I laughed. "You'd never do anything bad." Out of the four of us, she was the least likely to get into any trouble.

"But just in case."

"I'll do it," Terry said.

I shrugged. "Me too."

We looked at Aletta.

She frowned. "What do we have to lie about?"

"I don't know yet," Dorcas said.

"All right."

Dorcas smiled and then her face grew serious and her gaze slowly went around the room as if assessing us. "You have to keep the lie or else."

Aletta sniffed. "Or else what?"

"You'll die."

She was a silly girl, but so were we and very dramatic back then. We'd read several English classics that told of undying loyalty and they added some adventure to our dull, ordinary lives. "We'll keep it," Terry said. Aletta and I nodded.

Dorcas' smile returned. Then she took out three marbles and held them in the palm of her hand. "I'll give one to each of you when I want the promise kept."

When I think of it now, I don't know whether to laugh or cry. How silly it was that we'd later do something so dangerous for a promise and a ritual of receiving a marble we'd discussed as children. I quickly forgot about it. I was sure all of us did. I was wrong.

AFTER THAT RAINY DAY, our thoughts turned to boys and dreams of leaving Jamaica. Well three of us dreamed about it, Aletta never did. She thought it was the height of foolishness and a waste of time. None of us saw her leaving and for years she didn't. She ended up working in town as a teacher at a private school. However, the rest of us did dream. Terry said a sailor would come and whisk her away. Instead she married a clerk who took her to England and she had two children.

Dorcas did once say she'd marry a man who'd take her off the island far away to England. And surprise, she did finally meet some man who'd said he'd take her. He was a good worker, simple, but kind and I've nothing against that. She was so happy, boasting how he was going to take her to Cambridge and how much she'd learn there. But the Cambridge to which he took her wasn't the one in England. It wasn't even close. It was in Massachusetts. Yes, he took her to America. She never did see England. None of us had thought of going to America, a place where they mangled the English language so much so sometimes one wasn't sure they were speaking English at all.

I married too. A man who took me off the island and settled us in Canada. I was lonely, I admit it, and the gray days settled heavy on my soul, but I loved my husband and our growing family.

Terry kept in touch with all of us. She was like the glue that tied us together. Her letters were always a welcome sight in the post box. She was so full of life, we didn't expect the cancer to take her so quickly. Her husband was unable to cope, and her parents were dead and none of her siblings wanted two extra mouths to feed, leaving her two little ones all alone. Dorcas offered to take them in, even though she'd been newly married. Lucky for her, her man didn't mind.

In the seventies, my husband's job took him to

Virginia where I reconnected with Aletta. She'd married and divorced. She never mentioned her ex-husband and I never asked. Two years later Dorcas and her family moved to Maryland and we had a reunion. We gathered at my house because I still had the best food and the perfect space. I felt as if nothing had changed and half expected Terry to come through the door. And, for one brief moment, I thought she had when Deena, one of her daughters, came to greet me and then the other one, Lois. They both had their mother's beauty and kind, cheery nature.

Dorcas also had two little girls Michaela and Teresa—not pretty mind you—but sweet. She did dress all four girls as if they were princesses and doted on them. Her husband did too until him up and die on her only twenty-five years into the marriage. Fortunately, he left them enough money, which allowed the girls to educate them-selves and find proper men to marry. Terry's two girls had no problem and both married right after college. It took another decade for Dorcas' eldest daughter to do so, but she did at last. Her younger daughter had a devil of time finding the right match (I even considered my own son for her, but my husband laughed at the idea). She was not only plain but shy, her mother prayed for a man to see her for who she was and she eventually did catch one. A fine looking man.

Aletta was sour, as usual, at the wedding. "I don't like him eyes," she said.

She always said strange things like that. "His eyes are

fine," I said, wishing that Dorcas' daughter could have made a prettier bride.

"Then why him look 'pon the bridesmaids instead of the bride?"

I didn't know what to say. Michaela looked so happy and I was glad she was spared the lonely state of being single. A woman should marry. And if the man can be handsome that's good. "Don't make up stories."

"I'm not."

I ignored her and looked at Dorcas. She glowed. Six months later that glow was gone. I'd spotted her in a local shop and waved, but she looked right through me. I walked up to her and nudged her.

"Yuh not see mi wave?"

"Mi sorry I have troubles 'pon mi mind."

"What troubles?"

"Deena, is worried about Michaela and I haven't heard from her either. I have to see what's going on."

"How long has it been?"

"Two weeks."

"No need to worry."

"She calls me every week and we come here. Last time she told me she was sick and I asked if I could go see her and she said no. This time she didn't call."

"They're newly married. Perhaps she wants time alone."

"No, something's not right. That's not my daughter."

"She's a grown woman now."

Dorcas didn't listen to me. "Come with me."

———

Michaela lived in a lovely colonial house. Her new husband made a handsome income. It still surprised me that such a plain girl could have gotten herself a man who was both handsome and well off. But she was a good soul, so I was happy for her. What I didn't like was the garden, it was choked by weeds and I know Michaela wouldn't have allowed that to happen. Dorcas knocked. It was few moments before someone came to the door.

"Who is it?" Michaela asked.

"It's me darling," Dorcas said. "Your Mum."

Michaela seemed to hesitate then she opened the door.

I screamed first then her mother after me or it may have been the other way round, I'm not quite sure. But I do know that when I saw Michaela's face I let out a sound I didn't know I could make. I couldn't recognize her. And at that moment we knew that the fine looking man with a slow smile had a quick temper. He'd kept that temper well hidden. No one knew about it until that day.

Michaela looked around like a frightened mouse, pulled us inside and closed the door. "What do you want?"

"We wanted to see you."

"What happened?" I demanded.

Michaela lowered her gaze. "I was clumsy."

We knew that was a lie. She may look as dull as dishwater but she had the grace of a swan. "He did this to you?"

"He'll be home soon. You can't be here. Go."

"I can't leave you here."

"It will only make him angry. Please Mummy."

"No. Get your things."

"I can't leave him. He loves me. I just made him angry."

I stiffened with anger. "Your father never touched you and you let a man you lay with do this?"

Dorcas touched my sleeve to calm me. "You won't come with me?"

"No. It won't happen again."

"He promised you that?"

She nodded. Michaela froze when she heard a car door close. "He's home early. Don't say anything. Please."

I opened my mouth, but again Dorcas touched my sleeve, this time with more force. "We won't." She went into the living room and sat down, as if nothing had happened. That was how Michaela's husband found us when he came in carrying two dozen red roses and a gold necklace. I smiled at him and had to admit that Aletta had been right. I didn't like his eyes either.

———

A YEAR later Michaela gave her husband a son and four months after that he put her in the hospital with three fractured ribs, two black eyes and a broken nose. By that time it had become a family crisis. Dorcas' three daughters, Aletta and myself got together in the waiting room wondering what to do next.

"You see how he eats," Dorcas said. "That could work in our favor."

Aletta frowned. "How so?"

"A man like that can be poisoned."

Deena shook her head. "She wouldn't have the nerve."

"And it's against God," Aletta added.

Dorcas raised her voice. "Don't talk to me about God, when a man like that can be deacon in a church and not be struck down by lightning the moment he enters."

"There are other ways to get her away from him."

"She's too afraid. He said he'd kill her."

"She has to go to the police."

"Someone has to convince her."

"I will," Deena said.

And to my surprise she was able to persuade Michaela to press charges.

I held Dorcas' hand throughout the trial and Hudson's acquittal. Yes, the judge let him go because of his slow smile and charming ways. He said that hitting a woman was common where he came from and that he didn't know American ways and wouldn't do it again. He told lies about Michaela and made his actions seem justifiable. He walked out. Dorcas didn't move. But she began to smile.

"Yuh gone mad?" I asked her.

She only stood and turned to leave.

———

Michaela tried to get a divorce, but Hudson wouldn't let her. He threatened to take full custody of their son.

Dorcas went through her savings, trying to help her daughter with her legal fees. But no matter how disappointing the defeat, Dorcas' smile never left her.

"She has me worried," I told Aletta one evening after Dorcas had left us. We'd just had tea together at Aletta's flat. We usually meet at my house, but for some reason my husband decided to catch a cold and stay home that week.

"It's that smile," Aletta said.

"You noticed it too?"

Aletta set her tea cup down with a clatter. "How can you miss it?"

"If you didn't know her, she just looked calm and happy."

"Yes, but we do know her," she said, her tone grave.

"What could it mean?"

"I don't know." Aletta sighed. "But she worried me with her talk about God."

"She was just angry."

Aletta shook her head. "And yet she smiles."

I thought about that smile all night and I thought about it even more the next week when Hudson went missing.

Dorcas came to my house and the smile was gone, but her candyfloss voice was pleasant. "If anybody asks. I was *not* with you and Aletta last Thursday."

I still remember the cool round feel of the marble as she placed it in my hand.

———

"Did you get it?" Aletta asked me that night, her voice tense.

"Yes. You?"

"You gone daft? Why would I be asking you if I hadn't?"

"We must do as she asked us," I said.

"It's not right. She was with us. Why should we lie?"

"We made a promise."

"We were children," Aletta countered.

"Doesn't matter."

"She won't change her mind. I've tried."

"What if we don't?"

"Do you want to risk it?"

I remembered Dorcas' words that we would die if we broke our promise. I didn't believe it, didn't want to, but an icy shiver of fear swept through me. "No."

Aletta sighed. "I wonder why she's asking us to do this now."

Two weeks later we found out. A body was found burned beyond recognition. Through dental records it was identified as Hudson. Dorcas confessed to the murder. She admitted to poisoning Hudson and then dumping his body and setting it alight. Naturally the police were skeptical. How could a woman of Dorcas' age and build have carried his body to a clearing and then torched it? However, no matter how long they questioned her, she didn't waver. The police were certain Michaela was somehow involved, but they could find no evidence to support their suspicions and she had a solid alibi--a broken wrist that Hudson had given her--that had sent her to the ER. Dorcas gave no other names and took full responsibility.

Michaela was just as distraught by her mother's confession, but there was an air of resignation when I visited her. Her plain little face was eerily composed. Her broken wrist in a sling. I helped care for her son and tidied up her place. When I glanced out the window I was surprised to see her garden was blooming. All the weeds were gone. I wondered how she had managed that after surviving such a severe beating.

Dorcas was indicted and later convicted. I remember the look between Deena and Dorcas and I thought of Michaela's garden and how the weeds were gone. I knew that Michaela couldn't have tended to the garden herself, and how as children Deena and Michaela had been so close, just as their mothers had been. Although they were not related by blood their souls, at times, seemed to be as one.

Although, I didn't want to, I imagined Deena being angered by Michaela's latest hospital visit and deciding to do something to stop him. I imagined her poisoning Hudson and then discarding the body somewhere. I imagined Deena telling her mother what had happened and Dorcas coming up with a plan. I imagined Dorcas burning his body. But of course, that's all just an old woman's conjecture. What could I know of such things? The truth could be vastly different.

The investigation is closed, but I know the truth: Dorcas was with us the night Hudson disappeared. But it's a secret I have to keep. I won't dare let it escape, even though I hate keeping it. Besides, it's not such a stretch to believe Dorcas' story. Everybody knows that Dorcas Mortag burns everything she touches.

the one certainty

the one certainty

SHE HAD A CAT.

A large black and white ragamuffin she called Rossetti because she'd been reading one of Christina Rossetti's poems ('Remember' or 'Shut Out' she wasn't sure of the exact title but knew it was something that suited that somber Sunday afternoon awash in the scent of a cool summer rain) when the scraggly wet ball of fur showed up on the doorstep of her brick townhouse.

Strays were unusual since most animals got lost or eaten in the dense forest of trees out back that had been undeveloped for years and provided the view she craved since moving from Georgia to Maryland for a job that had seemed heaven sent after years of searching.

The cat was skittish at first, with reason Sylvia would soon discover. She'd been abused and the extent of her hard life was revealed when Sylvia managed to catch her and take her to the vet. She was a young cat, only about three years old, but she needed lots of care. To Sylvia's surprise her new roommate seemed hungrier for attention than food. It didn't take long for Sylvia to gain the cat's trust and she soon took treats from Sylvia's hand and talked when she felt the need, a soft cry, the scent of chicken in cheese gravy on her breath, but gaining attention was her biggest occupation.

Nudging Sylvia's thigh to get stroked, pawing her knee to get brushed; sitting by her side when she watched TV or worked. Sylvia had had a cat once when she was a child, a cute little grey short haired that preferred her brother to her and kept to herself and only came to Sylvia if she had food in her hand.

Rossetti was nothing like that. She didn't fit the description of the aloof, solitary temperament of most of her kind. She was very affectionate and purred the moment Sylvia entered the room as if her presence was enough. Soon they were inseparable.

Sylvia posted pictures of them together online: Trips to the seaside, the park, on long drives, hiking and picnicking. And Sylvia was happy for five years, even though she wasn't supposed to be.

She'd become a dreaded cliché without even knowing it. A single woman with a cat. No children. No man. Just a career she loved (she worked as director of a recreation center), a house she adored (split level with marble kitchen countertops and large windows) and a cat named Rossetti.

It was because of that oversight (How could you possibly be happy alone with just a cat? one friend had asked with a look of loving sympathy) that Sylvia started to date. It wasn't solely her idea of course, it was eagerly suggested and encouraged by her family and friends (the same ones who loved her cat pictures and followed her travel stories).

They warned her that she didn't want to be one of *those* women. And Sylvia believed them. She was far from being an eccentric Victorian spinster saved by the distance of both location and time plus, although there were blacks in England during that era, no one could stretch their imagination that far and label her that. But they did worry that her life was unnatural.

You don't want to be alone, they warned her.

Sylvia had never felt alone before. She'd never felt the loneliness that others wanted to save her from. A looming monster that hovered over singles and no one else. People in couples never felt lonely. The monster never consumed them. Others appeared to know best. They told her what to feel, how to feel since she didn't know on her own. How could she be happy?

She questioned herself. Doubted herself. Since others questioned her so often they must know something she didn't. They loved her and wanted the best for her, right?

Don't be too picky.

You're not getting any younger, they said.

She knew that. The passing of time had never bothered her before, but it bothered others. So she knew she had to act.

She wouldn't be a cliché any longer if she found someone to share her life with. She would put in the effort. Change her fate. Then everything would be perfect.

———

THE DATES WENT WELL.

Until they didn't.

I hate cats, I'm a dog man, one of her dates said, an astrophysicist who sniffed incessantly from allergies.

Then there was the physical education teacher who wanted to bike or run everywhere, including the grocery store where he liked to speed through the aisles (especially the produce section) and beat his previous time. And the businessman (she never quite understood what business he was actually in or what he did) was interesting, but then he disappeared.

The blind dates, online dates, speed dates and mixers were exhausting and she was about to give up when a friend of a friend introduced her to him.

The One.

The one who was good looking, charming, gainfully employed (he was an activities director at another rec center so they had that in common) and liked animals. They went wine tasting on their first date and many other dates followed. Sylvia settled easily into coupledom.

She didn't mind that sometimes he didn't like what she wore. A casually tossed remark, Are you sure you want to wear that? became frequent enough until she soon felt unsure. Was there something wrong? She'd been dressing herself competently for most of her thirty-one years, but he made every choice seem new again. She never realized that her green sweater wasn't a good choice with her black skirt. That her light cream blouse didn't have the right cut for a woman of her stature. Yes, she was kind of hippy and busty, she'd never really noticed how much before. She was happy to learn.

He talked about her weight only because he cared about her so much, he told her so many times and he sounded so sweet. So loving. He wasn't putting her down. He had a sister who suffered from diabetes and he was worried about her. Don't be so sensitive, he'd said. Or had she told herself that? She wasn't sure.

But she didn't want to be too sensitive. She didn't want to take his words the wrong way. She didn't want to be alone again. This was what being in a relationship was. You look out for each other. Ask questions.

Are you really sure you want to eat that? He asked on more and more occasions, usually in public.

One time Sylvia found herself looking down at the menu in front of her second guessing the linguini and scallops she'd told the waitress she wanted. She hesitated and felt a note of relief (or was it irritation? Worry? Fear?) when he ordered a spaghetti with cherry tomatoes for her instead.

She had been sure until he asked her. She'd been sure of herself for years. But now...now she was part of a couple and couples looked after each other, right? But when she teased him about his weight (the former Marine had packed on some pounds), she remembered the hard look in his eyes. How he met her light laugh with a glare. He said he was always a Marine and he didn't talk to her for nearly a week after that. He wouldn't reply to her texts, calls, messages or emails of apology. When he finally contacted her again, he said he'd been busy, but she knew better. She never teased him again.

SHE WAS LUCKY. That's what her friends kept telling her. She'd gotten a 'good one', which sounded a tad archaic to her modern ears, but she'd been pleased.

Her friends envied her and it was better to be envied than pitied so she didn't say anything about some of the things that bothered her about him. He was a 'good one'.

No one noticed that she no longer posted as many travel pictures as she used to. Or that her smile was different. They only noticed the man by her side. The man who seemed to always be by her side and they felt happy for her.

Even at a dinner party when he interrupted her, making her mute in front of a crowd, no one noticed, although she did. Sylvia made excuses for him, she'd gotten good at that, and her friends laughed and nodded in understanding. That's what you do, you compromise, her friends said.

Only Rossetti knew that Sylvia wondered if it was right. If she was truly happy or just pretending. Only Rossetti knew her conflict and the cat seemed even more eager to get Sylvia's attention. She hated to see Sylvia leave and curled up next to her extra tight at night, her soft purrs lulling Sylvia to an uneasy sleep.

Did she settle on him? Perhaps. Maybe because she was bored or just tired of looking. He made the questions stop (Are you really happy? How can you be happy alone?) and there was a victory in that. She was no longer in danger of living a dreaded cliché. Having a man changed that. His presence was a shield against the world.

Until it wasn't.

Until it was a prison.

No one noticed it until too late.

He was subtle. Dangerous changes always are.

He was very romantic. Except on the days he wasn't. The days Sylvia couldn't tell anyone about because she was one of the lucky ones now. She had a man. That was all that mattered.

———

HE DIDN'T LIKE POETRY. His disdain for the art form was almost violent.

He didn't like Rossetti and Rossetti didn't like him.

She never drew her claws or hissed at him, but when he came into the house, his polished black shoes echoing on the wood floors, she flattened her ears and kept her body low to the ground as if he were prey she was stalking. Prey she wanted to pounce on and devour. But she never moved close to him, never allowed him to stroke her, although he tried. He called to her, brought her treats and toys and smiled when he saw her. He said he liked animals and had owned two cats as a child.

Rossetti didn't care.

Sylvia made excuses for her, just as she did with him, saying that Rossetti was a stray and that she may not be used to men. Rossetti was never happy when he spent the night. Sylvia could hear her pacing outside the closed bedroom door. Once Sylvia had opened it to let Rossetti in, but he had been so upset (Not angry just upset, he was quick to explain. I'm just not comfortable. I'm sorry, Sylvie) that she never did it again.

Sylvia thought with time things would change. That Rossetti and him would get on better.

They never did.

Her friends kept telling her how fortunate she was even as they slowly fell away and emptied out of her life so that he could take up more and more of her space and time.

Maybe if she'd said yes to his proposal he wouldn't have gotten so angry. Maybe if she hadn't asked for more time, some space, he wouldn't have acted the way he did. Then she wouldn't have seen his other face.

When he came over for dinner a week after he'd asked her to marry him, it was the first time Rossetti had hissed at him. That should have alerted her that something was different about this night.

About this man.

A man she'd known for six months. Someone she thought she'd known intimately. But a stranger had arrived on her doorstep that cool autumn night.

A stranger filled with rage.

She didn't see it while it simmered during the appetizer. She'd made his favorite bake potato skins. She didn't see it boiling during the main course, another one of his favorites—something hot and fried. She'd blocked out the memory now, but the scent of paprika would always make her gag afterwards. She'd made the meal especially for him (was it because of guilt because she wasn't sure she wanted to marry him yet? Maybe. She still didn't have a solid answer for him, but a way to a man's heart was through his stomach and she hoped to pile it high with love).

He ate without saying much, which was unusual. He usually had a lot to say. He usually had an opinion about everything. She liked that about him. He was smart, engaging.

But that evening only the sound of a knife scraping across the white plate filled the room. Long, slow scrapes as he methodically shoved food in his mouth and cleaned his plate.

Sylvia smiled. Pleased that he'd enjoyed the meal so much. She opened her mouth to ask if he wanted seconds when he picked up the plate and smashed it in her face.

She fell backwards, hitting the ground hard. Tasting the blood from her busted lip, her bleeding nose. A silent scream trapped in her throat.

He wasn't done.

He came at her with the knife. Shoving the tiny square table aside, rattling the once carefully arranged dishes, determined to get to her.

She saw a flash of black and white leap through the air. Sylvia wasn't sure what it was at first until she heard him scream then she knew.

Rossetti went for his face. He stumbled backwards, fighting her. The wild creature didn't let go. Until he managed to grab her and throw her to the ground. She hit the sideboard and didn't move.

He turned his rage on the still form and raised the knife.

Sylvia grabbed the tureen and hit him with it.

It wasn't hard enough to make him go down, just stunned him and increased his rage. He spun towards her.

She saw his intent shining in his eyes.

He planned to kill them both.

She didn't plan to die.

She fought, struggled, prayed as she felt the knife penetrating her flesh. She bit him, clawed him, kicked him, but his rage gave him power.

But I love you, she said, her words ripping from her throat, echoing her confusion. How could he do this to her? Didn't he love her too? Hadn't he wanted to marry her?

He didn't answer. She didn't think he heard her, or no longer cared.

Sylvia looked up into a face she'd never seen before. Eyes that expressed nothing. Her shield, her safety was an illusion.

She'd learned that too late. She wasn't lucky. And now she had no friends left to witness that.

She turned her face away ready to die.

Then she heard a cry and a yelp both animalistic—one from a cat the other from a monster.

A renewed strength entered her. No, she wasn't alone. She had Rossetti. Sylvia saw the small white and black cat biting into the monster's flesh, scratching at his skin; it gave her enough time to act.

She escaped his grasp and made it outside, the rush of cold air brushing against her skin in a whisper. She saw the sight of a lit jack-o-lantern sitting on her neighbors' stone steps smiling like a ghoulish beacon of safety.

———

She survived but not without scars. Not without nightmares. The stitches and the surgeries reminders of what she'd endured.

He cried in the courthouse.

He cried when he was convicted. He told her how much he loved her. How she didn't understand. He hadn't been himself. He loved her so much. He blamed his actions on combat—on a flashback. He asked for her forgiveness and for a moment she saw the man she'd let into her life and heart.

A heart he'd tried to stop.

But in the courtroom she didn't see the monster of that night. Just an ordinary man. A 'good man'. A man who was supposed to keep her from becoming a cliché. And she felt tears stream down her face.

———

SHE MOVED from the house she'd adored and the job she'd loved. She settled into a new town and slowly made friends. People who didn't know anything about her past. And as the years passed, people teased her about her cat, Rossetti, who'd also survived the attack with scars and followed her like a shadow.

These new friends wondered when she'd go out and meet someone. She was fun and attractive they told her. She shouldn't be alone. She always smiled and said nothing.

There was nothing to say. She knew something she hadn't known back then. Slowly, as she started to post new pictures of her and Rossetti on their travels together her joy returned, she pushed past the darkness of the past.

She realized she wasn't broken. She never had been. She hadn't needed a man to fix her life, to save her from her singleness. She wasn't alone. She wasn't unhappy. When the right man appeared he would know that too.

For now...for always...she was grateful. There were few things she was certain of but she was certain of this: She had her life. Her freedom. She had a cat named Rossetti. A cat that had been there for her when no one else was. A cat that loved her no matter what and filled her heart with joy. She was a single woman with a cat.

And that was more than enough.

wrong turn

wrong turn

WANNA DIE, bitch?

Beth Wilcock hurried to her car, the cold breath of winter seeming to laugh at the attempts of the heat seeping through the large vents in the underground parking garage. The January weather seemed determined to make its presence known and the slightly chilled air touched her cheeks with icy cold fingers, making her shiver. Or it could have been because of the phone call from last night. She didn't want to think about it too much.

Wanna die, bitch?

But she couldn't stop herself. She knew that voice. Feared it. The first time she'd heard it, she'd dismissed it as just a crank call. She figured it was some drunken kid calling from the university close by. The Virginia suburb where she lived and worked had suffered an ice storm that had closed businesses for three days, people had gotten bored and pranks weren't uncommon.

Then it happened again.

And again.

And again.

For weeks.

He always started with the same three words; the same low male voice. He didn't try to disguise it. As if he wanted to taunt her. As if he wanted to say "I know who you are, but you'll never know me."

"Why are you doing this?" she'd once asked him.

He never gave her an answer. Or a reason. He took pleasure in her fear. He also took pleasure in her anger. When she shouted at him, using the foulest language she could think of, he just laughed, and it sounded like the thudding echo of nails being driven into a coffin—final, cold, deadly.

She hadn't gone to the police yet. The calls were short and varied. She had no proof, just her suspicions of who she thought he was. She knew the police would suspect the wrong man—the rapist who was stalking women in the metropolitan area, who stalked his victims first.

No, her caller was different. He targeted her with precision. He left messages.

He never did at first. He only started when she stopped answering his calls and he took it as a personal affront. He wanted her to suffer for an unknown crime. But she knew it was personal.

———

His name was Stephen York and she'd crossed him. She hadn't meant to. When she'd backed her little yellow sports car out of her parking space three months ago, she hadn't noticed his black sedan doing the same. She felt the bump then heard the sound of colliding metal and her heart sank.

She jumped out of her car and met eyes of ice, eyes of vengeance. Her heart didn't sink further, it shriveled. She'd seen him occasionally in the office complex where she worked in marketing, doing her best to avoid him and the rumors that surrounded him.

Martin Weston, the security guard, had arrived quickly on the scene to diffuse any issues. Everyone knew Stephen York meant trouble. He was the ruthless CEO of a finance firm, a tall black man who walked with the casual lethal arrogance of a gangster dressed in a businessman's suit. What would have been a minor altercation between others would be a declaration of war to him. She'd apologized profusely, even tried to turn it into a joke taking all the blame and saying that she'd pay. He didn't smile, instead saying "I know you'll pay."

She'd laughed at that (she still didn't know why since it wasn't funny) but she now knew she shouldn't have. She hadn't taken it seriously. She should have and had regretted it since. She knew what he was capable of. She'd seen him attack a stranger who'd just tapped him on the shoulder and later found himself pressed against the wall. She'd watched him shatter a mirror with his fist on the mezzanine level of the building. She'd hurried into the elevator before the guard approached him.

The mirror had been replaced the next day and nothing was said, but a man with a temper like that was dangerous. And now she knew how much. The calls had started soon after the car accident; she hadn't put the connection to him—thinking it had all been sorted—until she'd foolishly tried to cut in front of him in the cafeteria because she was late. In a low voice of warning he'd said, "You wanna die?"

She'd smiled nervously and laughed (again she didn't know why) and made sure to never cross his path again.

———

When Beth saw his car, she stopped as if his presence had suddenly loomed in front of her like a ghost. She didn't want to be alone. She would get security to escort her. She'd gain her proof soon, but not tonight. She went back inside.

When she requested an escort she was relieved to have Martin as the guard on duty; a black man who had sharp watchful eyes, and a calm quiet quality that she trusted. Not overly friendly, but not cold either.

"Glad it's you," she said as he walked her to her car. The air still felt chill, but not as deadly cold as before.

"Why?" he asked.

She shrugged, a little embarrassed. "Don't know, just need to feel extra safe tonight."

"That's what I'm here for."

She nodded, wishing she had something else to say. Because of her shyness, and her interest in him, she didn't always respond to him the way she wished. She wished she could laugh easily or chat without anxiety, but she couldn't. Others would think she was being rude or standoffish, but he didn't seem to mind.

She was almost to her car and knew there wasn't much more to say. Tonight she would be safe.

"Any plans?" he asked.

Would he ask her out? A little thrill went through her. At times she felt that he was interested in her too. If he did, she would say yes. "No, not really."

"I could make a suggestion."

Her heart started to pound. "Okay."

"Wanna die?" He stopped. "Bitch."

Her blood felt as if it had turned into a river of ice in her veins. At first she stopped just as he had, as if he had a cosmic connection that bound her to him. Then she heard a car door close from somewhere in the distance and she ran.

He chased her.

She screamed.

But the parking garage seemed to swallow the echoes of her voice. She darted between cars, feeling him coming in close behind her. She didn't look back, she ran until his footsteps didn't sound close enough and then she dropped to the ground and rolled under a car.

"I will get you," he said, sounding like the taunting voice on the phone. "You can't hide."

Why? Why? What had she done to him? She'd been kind. Always. She held her breath when she saw his shiny black shoes stop near her. They hesitated then moved away.

She didn't know how long she stayed their unmoving, barely breathing before she felt something grab her leg. A clamp—the clamp of a man's large hand wrapped around her ankle. He dragged her back, she clawed at the ground, her nails scraping against the cement, then she reached to grab the undercarriage of the car, but the wires she seized broke as he continued to drag her.

She emerged from the safety of the car and opened her mouth to scream. His fist stopped her as it made contact with her face.

He pointed at her, the expression of rage on his face one she'd never seen before. "Don't scream and I won't hurt you."

Beth didn't believe him. He'd already hurt her. She knew he'd do more.

She screamed again and felt the power of his fist against her cheek then saw darkness.

———

SHE KNEW THE ROOM.

Beth woke up, her legs and arms bound to a metal chair, her coat and handbag gone, and looked around her. She was in the storage closet on the top floor of the office building. She'd been there once before when Martin had helped her take some chairs to the conference room for a meeting. She'd never questioned why he had been there, perhaps she should have. Perhaps she should have wondered why he seemed to be around at the oddest times, showing up on her lunch break, bumping into her early in the morning, offering a 'hello' when she worked late. His actions had seemed harmless then. They had a more sinister tone now.

Why had he taken her there? Why did he hate her? What had she done? What did he want with her?

She closed her eyes when she heard the door open. The sound of his footsteps drew closer, soon followed by his taunting voice. "Wanna die, bitch?"

Is that all you can say? She wanted to scream but making him angry wouldn't help. She kept her gaze lowered, hoping she looked defeated.

"This is where I first fell for you," he said as if they were old lovers going down memory lane. "You were so pretty and shy and I liked that."

What changed? "I thought we were friends," she said, keeping her head lowered.

"Is that why you ignored me?"

When? "No I—"

"Are you calling me a liar now?"

Mustn't make him angry, must keep him calm. "No," she said quickly, lifting her head, but still keeping her gaze lowered. She wouldn't challenge him. "I'm sorry."

"You did. You ignored me because of him. You laughed when you were with him, you never laughed with me."

"Who?"

"You know who. York."

York? Never. "No, I don't like him. Never have."

He lifted her chin, forcing her to look at him. "Then how come when he said 'You wanna die' you smiled and laughed. I was there I saw it."

Beth stared into his dark, brown gaze wanting to see madness, but instead seeing a man made powerful by his own delusion. "I laughed because I was nervous. He always makes me nervous."

"And I don't?"

"No, because...I like you." She swallowed, trying to stomach her own lie. She had once, but not anymore. "You make me feel safe."

"Really?"

"Yes."

"Prove it."

"How?"

He untied her feet and hands then took a step back. "Stay with me."

"Okay," she said before she grabbed the metal chair and struck him with it, hitting him hard on the side of the face, knocking him to the ground.

Sharp pain surged through her when she raced to the door and closed it behind her. She briefly leaned against the door, gathering strength as she realized Martin had done something to her ankle, twisted or sprained it, she didn't know what, but she could imagine it now red and swollen. She didn't have time to examine it. She needed to get away from him.

Beth limped down the dark hall to the elevator that would take her to the main level since she couldn't make it by the stairs. When she reached it, she pressed the 'down' button multiple times urging it to come. *Please, please, please.*

In the distance she heard Martin banging on the metal door or was that her imagination? She wasn't sure. He could still be knocked out.

The elevator came. She stepped inside, gripping her hands together as the doors closed. She'd soon be safe.

She watched the numbers light up as the elevator car slowly descended. Then it stopped.

The doors opened.

Stephen York stood there.

Large, lethal, cold, but she'd been wrong. He hadn't been the voice on the phone. He hadn't been the one terrorizing her.

But she still didn't feel safe. Her mouth didn't move, although her heart screamed for help.

She watched him with wary eyes as he stepped onto the elevator and turned his back to her. He reached up and slammed the security camera with his fist, causing her to scream. She'd felt Martin's fists, she couldn't imagine what he could do to her. She was trapped.

"It's okay," he said, taking off his jacket. He held it out to her still not looking back. "You don't need to tell me what happened."

Beth reached for the jacket with trembling fingers. She was so cold, although the building wasn't.

"But you do need to call the police," he continued. "I'll wait with you until—"

"Why did you smash the security camera?"

"Because you kept looking at it terrified," he said in a

hard tone, but she preferred it to Martin's soft tones. "First I thought you were terrified of me, but then I knew I wasn't the one who'd attacked you, so I came to another conclusion."

I thought it was you at first, she wanted to say, but it was not the time to confess. She wasn't safe yet, Martin was still out there. "I can't be here," she managed, her voice hoarse.

"Why not?"

"Because he's still here in the building. I left him in the main storage closet on the—"

"I know where it is." The elevator doors opened. "I'll walk you to your car and then—"

"No, please don't—" She almost said 'leave me', but didn't want to sound as weak and helpless as she felt. York was the kind of man who didn't like weakness. "Don't get involved," she said following him out.

He turned to her as the elevator doors closed behind her. "Why not?"

"He's dangerous," she said then realized they hadn't gotten off on the main level, but had descended to the basement garage where Martin had attacked her. Despite Stephen's coat she still felt cold.

"Did he have a weapon?" he asked.

She shook her head. "He's part of security, he could find me."

"Will you let me drive you away from here?"

She nodded.

"Forgive me, but I'm not patient," he said then lifted her into his arms. "You'll slow us down."

Once inside the front seat of his car, Beth felt a semblance of safety, she'd soon be free from this nightmare.

Then the car wouldn't start.

Her mind flashed to the undercarriage and the busted wires. It was his car she'd hidden under? She'd ruined his car again? "This is my fault."

"No, it's not. There's another reason for this."

And her mind flashed to Martin's jealousy. Yes, he could have done something to his imaginary rival.

Stephen pulled out his cell phone. "Don't worry. I'm not going anywhere until he's in custody."

———

BUT MARTIN WASN'T where she'd left him. He had escaped and disappeared, cleverly avoiding all the security cameras. The police had arrived swiftly but there nothing they could do except search for a man whose mother said he was the sweetest child she had.

For four months the calls stopped, although her fear didn't.

Beth never worked late and every evening Stephen escorted her to her car. As time passed, she got to know him better. She learned that he did have a temper, but it was never violently out of control with others. When she'd seen him smash the mirror on the mezzanine he'd just received a call that his sister had lost her battle with her opioid addiction. He'd seen his reflection and blamed himself. He'd quickly apologized to the guard and paid for the damages. The stranger he'd assaulted, hadn't been a stranger at all, but an old college friend who he liked to roughhouse with.

He didn't smile easily but that didn't mean he was humorless and his statement in the cafeteria had been his way of teasing her. He was not dangerous. All her perceptions about him had been wrong and that shamed her the most.

Months later, when they were dating, she still couldn't tell him that she'd first suspected him. She didn't know why. A year later as she straightened their wedding photo that hung in the hallway of their new blue and white split level house she wondered if she could start to feel normal again. Start to fully forgive herself.

Then the phone calls began again. She'd been in the kitchen finishing off another piece of chocolate Stephen had gotten her for Valentine's Day when her cell phone rang. She hadn't checked the number, just licked her chocolate covered fingers and answered the phone.

Wanna die bitch?

She froze.

"What is it?"

Beth spun around at the sound of Stephen's voice behind her. She dropped the phone. She wasn't safe and now neither was he.

He saw her face and didn't need her to say anything. His expression darkened and he bent to pick up the phone, but she kicked it out of reach. He stared up at her surprised.

"I'm sorry," she said then hugged him.

He gathered her close and held her tight. "There's nothing to apologize for."

She mumbled something into his shirt.

He drew back and stared down at her. "What?"

"I thought it was you," she said in a choked whisper, shame and regret heavy in her voice. "At first I thought the phone calls were from you. I'm sorry."

He tenderly cupped her face in his hands and stared at her with the same expression of love in his eyes he'd had when he'd asked her to marry him. "It's okay."

But it wasn't. She had more to lose now. She didn't want to see him get hurt.

"Let me disappear until this is over."

"No, I'm not leaving your side."

———

But he wasn't by her side when a man's right hand washed up along the shores of the Chesapeake Bay. The police were able to identify it as belonging to Martin Weston, but the rest of him was never found.

Beth wasn't sorry, but she did wonder. She sat next to her husband as they watched a movie several weeks after the gruesome discovery and questions filled her mind. Did he know anything about it? She had wondered about his impromptu trip last week. And she hadn't seen him wear his peach colored shirt in a long while. Had he gotten rid of it? He did have eyes of vengeance. Was he capable of killing a man?

"What are you thinking about?" Stephen asked her, he had a habit of sensing when her mind drifted.

"Him. Martin."

"It's over now," he said in a soft voice.

She could only nod, feeling the weight of his arm as it rested around her shoulders.

"Do you believe me?"

She nodded again.

Stephen gently touched her cheek with the back of his fingers. "Martin was right handed, correct?"

"Yes," Beth said, remembering the savage blows he'd given her, her chest tight. "I guess he isn't anymore."

"No."

She stared at the TV screen unable to look at her husband, her mind whispering...*the devil you know is better than the devil you don't.*

He pressed his lips against her forehead they felt solid and warm against her skin. "He'll never hurt you again."

Beth felt the tension within her ease. No, Stephen York was no devil and she wouldn't spend any more time suspecting him—she didn't care what he had or hadn't done. She was safe now; her life was her own again. She would forgive herself, she'd committed no crime and she no longer needed to feel imprisoned. She turned, met his dark gaze and smiled, grateful she could finally breathe.

bonus story

Thanks to the support of Kickstarter backers this collection includes the bonus story "Regrets."

regrets

regrets

He knew she hated roses.

Especially pink ones with baby breaths.

He knew she hated blue tinted vases too.

And yet there they sat— a bouquet of pink roses accented by white baby breaths in a blue vase—on her dining room table. A sight as attractive to Maureen Aja as a bottle of Pepto-Bismol. After a hard day at the hospital, where she now worked as an administrator, this was the last thing she needed. She turned and heard something crunch beneath her feet. She glanced down at the cement floor, not covered by an area rug, and saw a broken pair of plastic utensils snapped in two.

He also knew she didn't like when he used plastic utensils. They had plenty of knives and forks at home. It didn't matter that the delivery person added them to the takeaway order, that didn't mean one needed to use them.

Maureen swore and picked up the broken pieces and threw them in the kitchen trash bin. The scent of the kung pao chicken he'd ordered still lingered in the air, the sound of voices from the TV the only sound in the room.

The flowers and utensils were only a few of the things her husband had been doing recently: Each action a silent but potent gesture of aggression.

Enough was enough. Maureen took a deep breath and glared at the sight of her husband eating from the takeaway carton in front of the TV. He wore jeans and a striped T-shirt he'd had since his university days. Although premature grey sprinkled his close cropped black hair, he hadn't changed much. But she had. There were few things she could fit from years ago.

She folded her arms. "If you want a divorce just say it."

He kept staring at the TV and eating and saying nothing. He hadn't said much in weeks. Months. Neither had she. Not since...

Was it possible to hate how someone chewed? She looked at his jaw and heard the crunch of the fried wonton strips he seemed to add to every Chinese dish along with enough hot sauce to make your eyes bleed.

She let her hands fall to her sides. "Okay, you win. Do you want me to leave? Just say it and I'm gone."

He didn't look at her just took another bite. Crunch. Crunch. Crunch.

"I hate you."

"Not as much as I hate you," he said around a mouthful of food.

Well at least he'd spoken. That was something even though it was barely coherent. It hurt, but she'd wanted to hurt him too, so it was fair. This was what eight years together had gotten them.

She sat down on the far end of the couch feeling suddenly tired and worn and hungry but he didn't look like he'd ordered enough for two and she wasn't about to ask him. She stared at the TV. She saw a Nollywood comedy he liked but one she'd found too far-fetched for her tastes. From his absolute love of Nollywood films—from comedies to dramas—one would have thought he'd had the same Nigerian background as her, instead of having ties to the Caribbean. She sat back and sighed in defeat. "We should have never gotten married."

"You shouldn't have proposed."

"You shouldn't have shown up for our first date."

"You shouldn't have laughed when the waitress got your order wrong."

"You shouldn't have helped me eat it."

"It was good."

"Yes, it was."

"I wish…"

"Me too."

It had been a long time since they'd been able to read each other's thoughts. The distance had grown so much between them. The walls so thick, she never thought a moment like this would happen between them again. The moment they'd agree about something positive.

She clasped her hands together. "Staying together hurts too much, doesn't it?"

He didn't agree. He didn't say anything. He shut her out again.

Her stomach growled. She ignored it, he did too. She hung her head. "We should never have met."

Silence.

She turned and looked at the ugly pink flowers. The sight made her stomach hurt. There was no way to avoid the sight of them in this small space. From the position of the couch you could see everything—the tiny dining table that seated two, the half kitchen, the bookshelf they used as a wall for their makeshift bedroom on the other side. She'd never imagined they'd end up living in his parents' unfinished basement. Two people in their thirties with university degrees should be starting a family, vacationing, redoing their kitchen cabinets. Not living like this. So much was wrong now.

Maureen unclasped her hands, rested them on her lap. "I'll move out."

Silence. Again.

But it didn't matter because it was a vague threat with no heat. She had nowhere to go. That was the problem. They were stuck with each other. They'd built a life together that had become so entwined, untangling it would cost money. Money they didn't have because...

He took another mouthful. Chewed then said, "Just say it."

"What?"

Silence. He wasn't going to help her because he knew what she'd been thinking.

"Why don't *you* say it?" she challenged him.

He shook his head.

She stood. "I'm going to bed."

"Aren't you hungry?"

"No," she said. Her stomach grumbled, revealing her lie, but she didn't take it back. Living a lie was something she'd grown used to.

———

HE CAME into their makeshift bedroom a few hours later. Considering how much they'd grown to hate each other it surprised her that they managed to still share the same bed. But if he could stomach it so could she.   Neither wanted to be on the bumpy couch. It felt as if a bunch of overeager kindergarteners had stuffed it with newspaper.

She wished she'd been asleep before he came. That way she wouldn't have to hear the soft sound of his breathing, notice the weight of his body when he shifted in bed, smell the minty scent of mouthwash. The man could swim in the amount of mouthwash he used every day.

Why was she still with him?

Why was he still with her?

It was getting unbearable.

They should end it.

One of them had to be brave enough to do it.

She kept waiting for it to be him.

———

THE NEXT MORNING, a crisp and cool grey day that matched her mood, Maureen got in her car—their car, the green Toyota with the dent on the left rear door, they'd been forced to sell the Porsche—took a deep breath then hit the steering wheel with her fist. That bastard! The car had the sickly artificial scent of pine trees. She hated the smell of pine trees!

She yanked down the air freshener, setting the rearview mirror askew, and marched back inside where he was sitting at the dining table eating a bowl of granola cereal. He worked from home so he could set his own hours.

Crunch.

Crunch.

Crunch.

She threw the air freshener on the table which had no impact because it barely made a sound. It was like throwing down a feather during a duel.

Maureen took a deep breath. She wouldn't shout, although she wanted to scream. "What is wrong with you?"

His gaze remained on the bowl. He took another spoonful.

Crunch.

Crunch.

Crunch.

"I want a divorce."

The crunching stopped.

Finally she had his attention. His full attention. He actually looked at her, which mildly surprised her. She'd started to forget what color his eyes were. She knew they were brown, but they were a musty kind of brown like wet sand.

"Why?" He pointed at her. "And don't tell me I know why. I want to hear you say it."

"That's not fair."

"What's not fair about it? Why won't you say it?"

She swallowed. She opened her mouth. Closed it. "I'm going to be late for work." She turned.

Crunch.

Crunch.

Crunch.

––––––––

SHE RETURNED HOME late from work. She knew he hated when she did that. She knew he hated when she didn't call, but if he could play this stupid game so could she. Why should she have to say anything? Why couldn't he end it for both of them? She'd asked for a divorce that had been the first step, why hadn't he just played along and agreed?

There was nothing to save.

––––––––

SHE ENTERED their basement apartment greeted by the scent of another takeaway meal, possibly Italian this time.

More plastic utensils.

More crunching. Breadsticks this time.

When was the last time he'd cooked anything? When was the last time they'd eaten together?

She hung up her coat.

"We should never have gone to Bermuda," she said.

"You shouldn't have worn that light blue dress," he countered.

She walked over to him, inhaled the scent of the spinach ravioli on his plate. She wouldn't ask for any. She'd scrounge for leftovers in the fridge. "It was green."

"It was blue with silver straps."

She paused. "Oh yeah. You remember that?"

He nodded, his voice quiet. "I do."

That night on the beach she'd told him she loved him. She'd told him first. She was the first to do many things. The first to call him after their first date (wasn't that against the rules or something?) The first to kiss him. The first to plan their first weekend away (He hadn't complained, perhaps that had been a sign?). The first to want to be exclusive, the first to lose her heart.

She set her keys on the coffee table. "Why did you marry me?"

"I was bored."

She looked down. The pain had become comfortable. Had he ever loved her? Probably not. Like everything else she'd made her declaration and he'd followed along.

Maureen felt the stinging of tears. It was too much. "Just say yes." Her words were a plea.

"To what?"

"A divorce."

"No."

She kept her gaze lowered. "Why not? You've agreed to everything else. I know what people say about us. You're so easygoing and you have to put up with me and my charging ahead. I bullied you into dating and then marrying me. Even starting a business had been my idea—"

"I've never done anything I didn't want to do."

She looked at him, curious. "So you have no regrets?"

"I didn't say that."

"Then say what you really mean."

"You first."

"Why me?"

"Because it matters."

Did it really? "I'm going to bed."

"Eat something first."

If only they hadn't gone to Bermuda. If only she hadn't listened to a handsome man with a tongue of honey. If only she'd seen the signs. "No."

Greg surged to his feet. "Say it!"

Maureen took a step forward to cover his mouth, but stopped herself before she touched him. "Shh! Do you want to wake up your parents?"

"Say it now! Stop torturing me like this."

Her voice cracked. "Torturing you?"

"You think I haven't noticed the late shifts, the missed meals, the sleepless nights? You think I don't notice the lost weight and the bags under your eyes? I know you're miserable. I know you hate the sight of me. I need you to say it. I need you to say what you've wanted to say for the past year."

She squeezed her eyes shut. She could say the words, but she couldn't look at him. She didn't want to see the anguish on his face. "I wish your brother was dead. I think he's no better than pond scum. I know you love him, but...that's how I feel. How I've always felt."

Silence.

Maureen opened her eyes.

Greg stared at her openmouthed.

His stunned expression confused her. "Why are you looking at me like that?"

He blinked quickly. "I-I didn't expect you to say that."

"What did you expect me to say?"

He shook his head. Rubbed the back of his neck, let his hand fall. "I don't know. But not that." He briefly covered his eyes before his searching gaze met hers. "This is about my brother?"

"Not just about him. About you too."

He stiffened.

"But you know that." She paused. "Now it's your turn. Admit it. You don't want me here anymore than I want to be here."

He shook his head again. "That's not true."

"You love your family. Especially your brother and you believe him over me. Money doesn't just disappear. He took it somehow."

Greg rested his hands on his hips. "It's not that simple."

Maureen gripped her hand into a fist. That's what

he'd said the first time she'd confronted him about the missing money.

It had been his brother's idea to start the beverage company based on one of Greg's popular mixtures as a beverage chemist. He'd convinced her first and then she'd convinced Greg in return. It had been a great idea and they were slowly building the business beyond local restaurants and small gift shops that stocked their product. She had such vision for their company before she'd gotten sick. "Then why did you betray me? We'd built the business together. We were doing well. When I got sick I told you not to trust him, but you did. You let him be in charge of the accounts, and instead of buying new equipment we needed to grow, he bought cheaper ingredients and then gambled away all the money."

Greg sighed. "Not all of it."

"Enough to sink us! Enough so that when I came out of the hospital there was nothing of the business left to save.

"We have nothing to show for all our efforts. We're never going to get out of this debt. I wish you hadn't hired your brother behind my back. He's always getting into trouble—"

"Not always."

"Remember the food truck you helped him with?"

"It would have worked if the market hadn't turned."

"How about the T-shirts he tried to sell?"

"He sold some."

"He's a dreamer."

"That dreamer gave us the idea for our business. He gave us the courage to start something on our own."

"And he then took it away from us."

Greg sighed. "It's not that simple."

"See? You're always protecting him." Maureen gestured to the room. "Look where that's gotten us."

Greg fell quiet for a moment before he said, "It was me."

"What?"

"The lost money. It wasn't my brother. It was me. I gambled it not him. He took the blame because...I knew it would be easier for you to hate him. But now you can hate me. I screwed up. I lost track of things, didn't buy the new equipment. I thought that if I used some less expensive ingredients we could make a bigger profit and...you know the rest."

Yes, they lost clients. Much needed cash flow.

"I made the bad decisions. I'm not as smart as you, but I fooled myself that I could make up for it."

She paused. That didn't sound right. She was far from a forensic accountant but when she'd frantically gone through the books to find out where the money had gone, buying cheaper ingredients hadn't been one of the issues. Telling him that it had been one of the reasons, had been a test, a way to find out what had really happened. Greg had always focused on quality, the customers trusted their brand. That hadn't been the reason they'd lost them. "No, you didn't."

"I did this time."

He was lying. Why was he lying?

She'd learned from a former client that the client had increased their orders but that their company had been unable to fulfill orders due to lack of resources. "You're still trying to cover for your brother, aren't you?"

"No." He sat down, faced the TV.

But she'd already seen the guilty look on his face. "What are you hiding from me? Where did the money go?"

"I failed you, okay? I failed you as a husband. That's what you really want me to say, right?"

Her heart began to pound. Greg rarely looked guilty. It wasn't in his nature. The last time he'd had that look on his face was when they'd first started dating and she'd learned he'd pawned his guitar to help her pay rent when her roommate had bailed on her. She'd been so angry at him when she'd uncovered the truth (when his brother had told her actually) that she'd found a way to buy the guitar back and told him not to do something like that again.

Maureen started to put the pieces together. The amount of medical bills for doctor's visits, prescriptions, surgical procedures, recovery. She'd never thought about how they'd managed to afford it all. She'd been so focused on getting well and working at their company again that she'd believed Greg when he'd said that their health insurance had covered it all.

She thought about the reason he'd brought his brother onboard to help in the first place and a new possibility revealed itself.

"You didn't."

The look on his face told her all she needed to know. It was the pawned guitar all over again except he'd used the funds to take care of her.

This was the first time in months that she'd allowed herself to think clearly. She'd been so desperate to hold onto their old life—their business—that she hadn't realized how quickly she'd clung to the story that the money had been lost. That the business hadn't been managed well. In her mind his brother had been the perfect scapegoat.

He'd gone into debt paying for her medical bills. She'd wondered how they'd managed to cover the payments. But she'd focused so much on how much trouble the business was in that she'd never considered it.

"Why didn't you tell me?"

He folded his arms. That was answer enough. He knew she'd have said no and he wasn't going to accept that.

Maureen looked around their basement apartment with a new horror. "This is all my fault."

"No, it's not. That's why I didn't tell you."

"If I hadn't gotten sick, you wouldn't have had to look after me, you wouldn't have had to have your brother come. You wouldn't have had to spend all the money. How much was the insurance willing to cover? You should have—"

Greg slowly rose to his feet. "They weren't going to cover the surgery and you needed that surgery. They..." He took a deep breath. "I tried to talk and explain that it was necessary but they wanted you to try a less expensive medical procedure first. We didn't have time for that. Not when your life was at stake. You wanted that surgery and I wanted it for you and I was going to make it happen no matter what. So yes, you can hate me for that. When it comes to you, I will lie, I will deceive, I will do whatever is necessary to make sure I've done my best for you."

"But—"

"I don't regret a thing. I'd do it all over again even if..." He paused, sighed. "Even if you decide to leave me right now. It was—is—worth it to see you angry. Because you're here." His voice cracked on the last word, he cleared his throat but his tone still held the weight of his emotions. "You're alive. Because the truth is I could face losing the business, the house, some friends, but I couldn't face losing you without a fight. The thought of you not..." He hung his head, lowered his voice. "I would have done anything. I don't regret a thing. Not one single thing."

She'd been so proud of what they'd built. It had become part of her identity. Her reason for living. Losing it had felt as if she'd lost herself. Most of her life had been focused on achievement. That was what had been expected of her and she meant to succeed. Getting the best grades, going to the best schools, marrying well, living in the best zip code had been her life's plan. That had driven her.

Getting sick hadn't been part of it. She'd made no room for it.

She remembered drilling Greg on the day-to-day

activities from her hospital bed. In spite of the doctor and nurses warning her that she should rest.

No wonder he'd lied to her. The business had been her greatest pride. He was right. She would have forgone the surgery she'd wanted, that had taken out the tumor, instead of waiting on the results of a medicine that hadn't been effective as quickly as the doctors had hoped in shrinking it. She would have told him the business was more important. But she *also* remembered telling him how much she'd wanted the experimental surgery. How much it had meant to her. She'd never imagined the lengths he'd have to go to make it happen.

"I'm sorry," she said. "I made you suffer so much. If I hadn't—"

"No, you did nothing wrong. I lied because I'd rather you hated me than yourself."

"Is that why you've been acting this way? The ugly flowers, the air freshener?"

"You'd started sleepwalking through life, going to work, coming home, taking pleasure in nothing but longing for the life we'd used to have. But you'd numbed yourself against it. Against me. I wanted you to feel something again, even if it wasn't something good. I wanted you to see me again. Really look at me."

She held his gaze. "I'm looking at you now."

"I know." He took a step closer but still kept his distance. "You are the greatest thing..." He paused. "I feel lucky to be here with you. You have every right to be angry."

Maureen closed the distance and took his hand. "I'm

not angry. I'm scared." She released a shaky breath, surprised she'd managed to say the words. "This isn't the life we'd planned. We're so far behind. Everyone is so far ahead of us. I don't think we can catch up."

Greg squeezed her hand, his tone earnest. "We don't have to catch up. I don't care about comparing our life to anyone else's. We just have to live. Life isn't a race. Life is just meant to be lived and every day I get to spend with you is a victory to me."

She bit her lip as she gazed at the man—the same man that time had barely touched—she'd fallen in love with on that beach in Bermuda. The weight of illness, debt, disappointment hadn't dashed her feelings for him. "I'd always wondered if..."

"If what?"

"If you loved me as much as I loved you."

His brows shot up. "There's no question I love you more."

Maureen shook her head and laughed. It had been a long time since she'd done that. "I don't think that's possible." She felt a renewed vigor enter. She suddenly saw possibilities again. He was right, it wasn't too late. "I want to start again. I know it will take effort but I want—"

"Okay."

She didn't have to convince him. He understood. He always understood. She wrapped her arms around his neck. "Marry me."

He shook his head with regret. "Sorry. I'm already married."

"Does your wife know how lucky she is?"

He pressed a kiss on her lips then whispered, "I think she's starting to figure it out."

"Yes." She sat down and grabbed his half-eaten food, hungry enough to eat the plate and utensils too.

He held his hand out. "Let me warm it up for you."

She playfully smacked his hand away. "Leave me alone." She ate several forkfuls before she leaned back and sighed, feeling no longer as worn and tired as she had been moments before."Delicious."

He sat down beside her and wiped some sauce from the corner of her mouth with his thumb.

She frowned and shot him a look. "I hate when you do that."

He sucked the sauce off his thumb and said, "I know," before his mouth softened into a smile.

about the author

Dara Girard, an award-winning, national bestselling author of more than fifty novels and many short stories, from romance to suspense, loves telling stories.

Born in the US to immigrant parents, Dara enjoys pulling from her Jamaican, British, Nigerian heritage and exposure to various cultures to bring what reviewers and fans call "vivid emotional stories" to life. She is best known for her popular Henson Series, the mysterious Clifton Sisters, and the fun Black Stockings Society.

Visit her website to sign up for her newsletter and get sneak peeks, monthly updates on new releases, and special offers.

For more information visit
www.daragirard.com

www.ingramcontent.com/pod-product-compliance
Lightning Source LLC
Chambersburg PA
CBHW030645190726
48286CB00008B/2663